W9-COE-270

Harvest Party!

by Jennifer O'Connell
illustrated by Mike Wohnoutka

SCHOLASTIC INC.

ISBN 978-0-545-87234-8

10 9 8 7 6 5 4 3 2 1   15 16 17 18 19

Printed in the U.S.A.   40
First printing 2015

Book design by Jennifer Rinaldi

For Brendan, with many
thanks for your words, wit,
and wisdom
—J.O.

To David LaRochelle and Cow
—M.W.

Where are the apples?
Where could they be?
Ten bushels sat
right under the tree.

Pssssst! Party tonight
when the moon shines bright.
We'll bob for apples—
can't wait for a bite!
. . . *but don't tell the farmers.*

Where are the pumpkins?
They're missing, too!
Now there's a space
where **nine** of them grew.

Pssssst! Party tonight
when the moon shines bright.
We'll make pumpkin pies
and they'll taste just right.
. . . but don't tell the farmers.

Where are the clothes
on the line outside?
Eight shirts are gone,
now, where could they hide?

Pssssst! Party tonight
when the moon shines bright.
We'll get all dressed up.
Won't we be a sight!
. . . *but don't tell the farmers.*

And where is our corn?
It's just as I feared.
Seven tall stalks
have all disappeared!

Pssssst! Party tonight
when the moon shines bright.
We'll pop all this corn—
a yummy delight!
. . . but don't tell the farmers.

Where are our flowers?
Where did they go?
Six different colors
were all in a row.

Pssssst! Party tonight
when the moon shines bright.
We'll spruce up the barn,
then close the door tight.
. . . but don't tell the farmers.

Where are the gourds
that hung from the fence?
All **five** have vanished,
it doesn't make sense!

Pssssst! Party tonight
when the moon shines bright.
We'll rattle these gourds
with all our might!
. . . *but don't tell the farmers.*

Where is the grain?
Who took our food?
Four bins are empty.
That's very rude!

Pssssst! Party tonight
when the moon shines bright.
We'll bake nutty bread
and savor each bite.
. . . but don't tell the farmers.

Where are the hay bales?
Where did they go?
Three were lined up
all in a row!

Pssssst! Party tonight
when the moon shines bright.
We'll dance on these bales,
till the morning light.
. . . but don't tell the farmers.

Where are the banjos?
They're not in their cases.
Our **two** banjos
have left their places!

Pssssst! Party tonight
when the moon shines bright.
We'll strum up a tune
and rock all night.

. . . but don't tell the farmers.

One key is missing!
It's gone from its hook.
Quick, to the barn,
let's go take a look!

Pssssst! Party tonight
when the moon shines bright.

Behind the barn door
we'll turn off the light . . .
And then tell the farmers—

Surprise!

Pigs pluck their banjos.
Goats munch on corn.
Cows dance the two-step.
A party is born!

The farm work is done
and we're ready for fun.
Happy harvest, everyone!